Lullaby for Emily

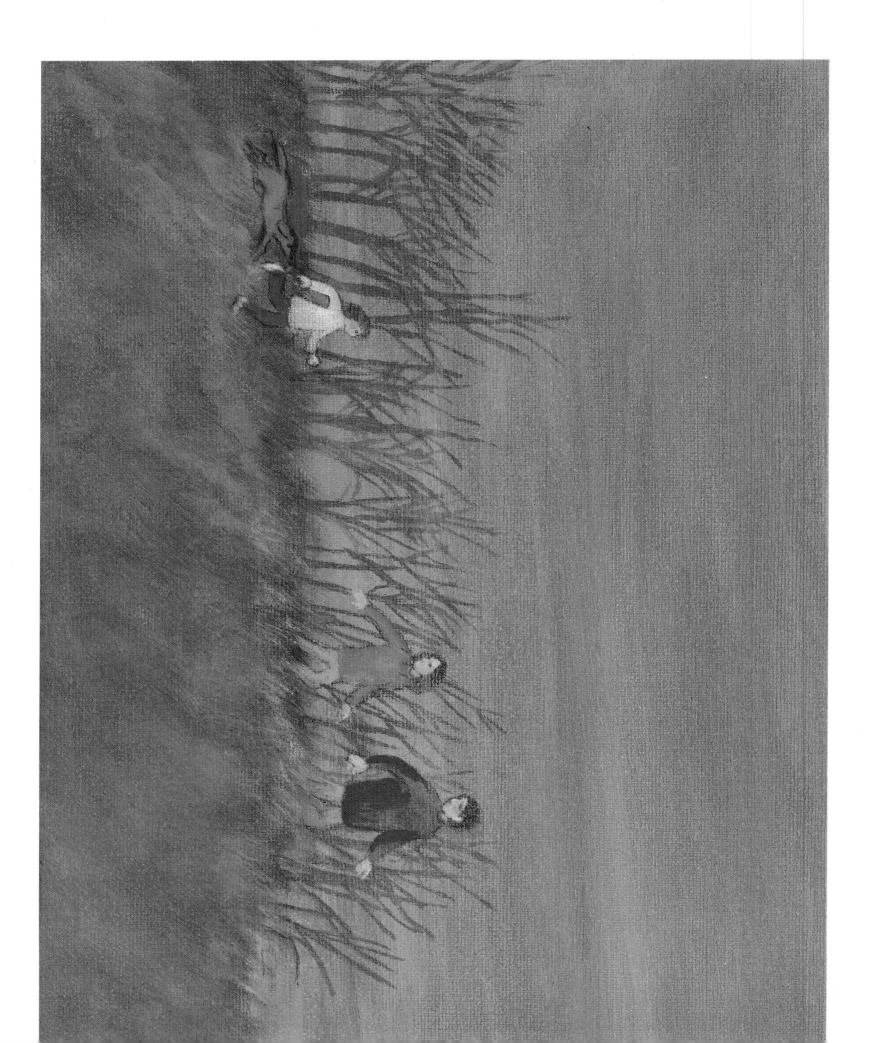

Lullaby for Emily

By David Kherdian ~ Pictures by Nonny Hogrogian

Henry Holt and Company
New York

Henry Holt and Company, Inc.

Publishers since 1866

115 West 18th Street

New York, New York 10011

Published in Canada by Fitzhenry & Whiteside Ltd.,
195 Allstate Parkway, Markham, Ontario L3R 4T8.

Library of Congress Cataloging-in-Publication Data

Kherdian, David.

Lullaby for Emily / by David Kherdian; pictures by Nonny Hogrogian.

Summary: A lullaby spoken to the soon-to-be-asleep Emily.

[1. Lullabies.]   I. Hogrogian, Nonny, ill.   II. Title.

PZ7.K527Lu   1995   [E]—dc20   94-6835

ISBN 0-8050-2957-5

First Edition—1995

The illustrations for this book
were prepared in oil on canvas.

Printed in the United States of America

on acid-free paper. ∞

1 3 5 7 9 10 8 6 4 2

Sleep gently, sweet Emily,
sleep softly, sleep well,
and when you awaken
we will go and watch the animals
and see what they are like,
the porcupine in the tree,
the skunk on the ground,

the masked raccoons at night,
stealing whatever can be found,
and listen to the barking fox,
the hooting bear that in the spring
sounds like the owls of the night.

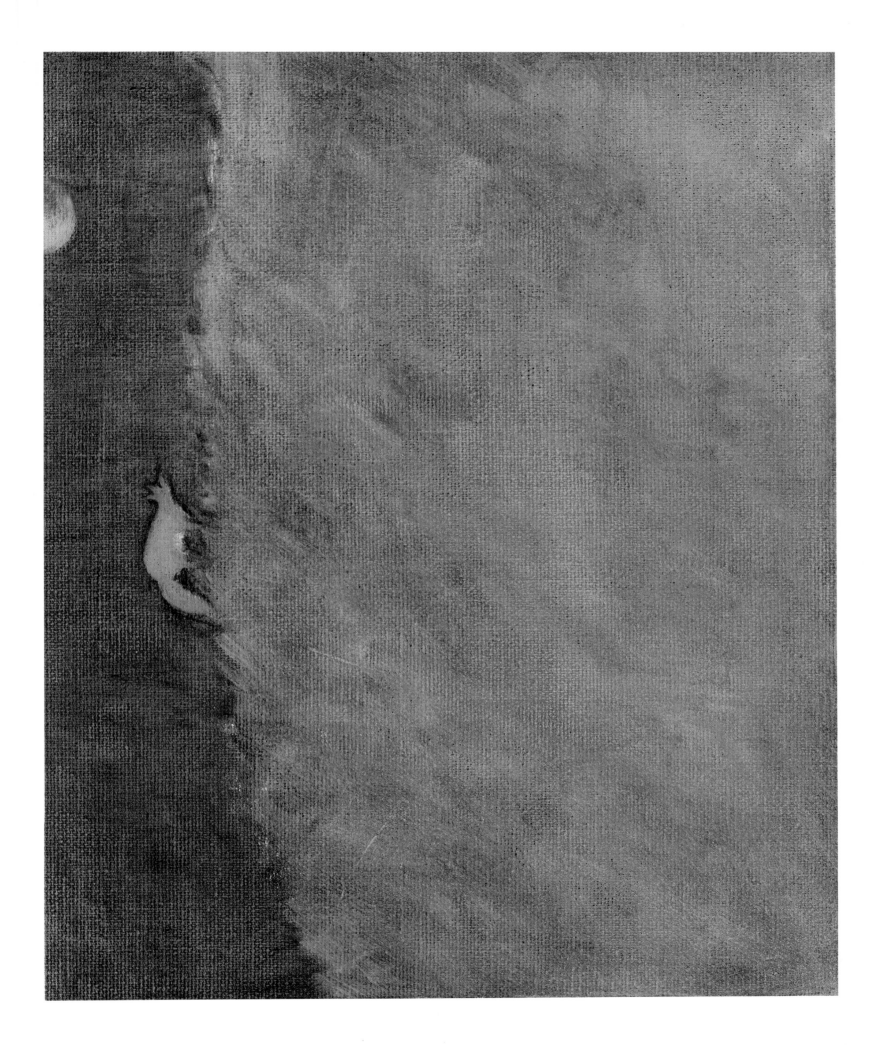

Sweet Emily, sleep gently,
we will build a bluebird house nearby,
and you can climb the linden tree
and listen to them sing,
for they are gentle, they are quiet,
and not easy to find.

Sweet Emily, sleep softly,
in the meadows the wildflowers
are blooming again,
blue and pink and yellow and white,
waiting to be gathered and taken home,
some for the vase in the parlor,
some for the glass beside your bed,
and others for making necklaces
and for plucking to see,
does he love me yes, or does he love me not.

Sleep softly, sweet Emily,
and we will plant a summer garden,
beets and string beans and Swiss chard too,
and hoe up the potatoes
and string the peas,
and watch the corn grow over our heads,
and the scarecrow needn't be afraid
of anyone,
not even you.

Sweet Emily, sleep gently,
and you will have your puppy
cuddly and warm
licking your face and pulling your sleeve,
and going with you everywhere you go,
because he is your pet,
and because you love him so.

Sleep gently, sweet Emily,
the blackberries are ripening all around,
so take the dog and make him bark
or the bears might come around,
and we will fill baskets and take them back home,
for cereal, for jams, for making pies,
and some to eat when we are all alone.

Sweet Emily, sleep softly,
for soon we will go swimming
beyond the beaver pond,
and if we are good and quiet
they might not be afraid,
and if we are lucky
we might see them at their play.

Sleep gently, sweet Emily,
we will play in the meadow
and jump in the hay
and bring the cows home,
that have been gone for the day.

Sleep gently, sweet Emily,
there are more apples on the tree
than have fallen down,
some for the deer and some
for us, some to make
cider and some to make sauce,
but none for the fox that
barks to another's sound.

Sweet Emily, sleep peacefully,
soon with your father you will go
to carry home kindling for the fire,
so put on your muffler, put on your gloves,
and I will prepare mulled cider
on the cooking stove while you are gone.

Sleep softly, sweet Emily,
there will be tobogganing on the hill
and skating on the pond
and snowmen to build,
and snowballs to make
to defend your fortress
against all who would challenge your town.

Sleep gently, sweet Emily,
for the warbler sings
to endings and beginnings,
to the light turning dark,
and the sun nearing the mountain
soon to be lost to sight,
sleep gently, sleep sweetly,
it is daylight, it will soon be dark,

sleep sweetly, sleep gently,
one day brings another,
there is no end to time,
sleep gently, sleep sweetly
for love is all around.